AFRICA AFRICA AFRICA AFRICA AFRICA AFRICA

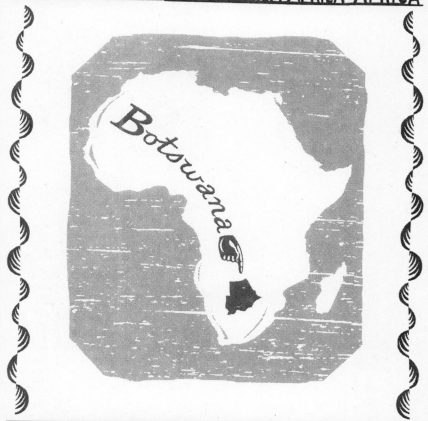

Botswana

AFRICA AFRICA AFRICA AFRICA AFRICA AFRICA

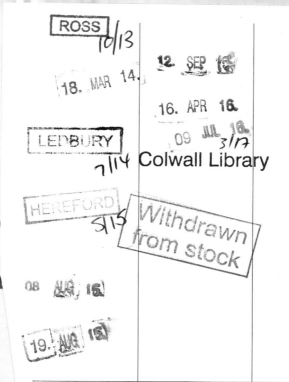
M
MI

Ale

Illus

First published in Great Britain in 2012
by Polygon, an imprint of
Birlinn Ltd
This Large Print edition published
2013 by AudioGO Ltd
by arrangement with Birlinn Ltd

ISBN: 978 1471 362057

Text copyright ©
Alexander McCall Smith 2012
Illustration and design ©
Iain McIntosh 2012

British Library Cataloguing in Publication Data available

Printed and bound in Great Britain by
TJ International Limited

CHAPTER ONE

This is the story of a girl called Precious. It is also the story of a boy whose name was Pontsho, and of another girl who had a very long name. Sometimes people who have a very long name find it easier to shorten it. So this other girl was called Teb. There is no room here, I'm afraid, to give her full name, as that would take up quite a few lines. So, like everybody else, we'll call her Teb.

Precious's family name was Ramotswe, which sounds like this— RAM–OT–SWEE. There: try it yourself—it's not hard to say. She lived in a country called Botswana, which is in Africa. Botswana is very beautiful— it has wide plains that seem to go on and on as far as the eye can see, until they join the sky, which is high and empty. Sometimes, you know, when you look up at an empty sky, it seems as if it's singing. It is very odd, but that is how it seems.

1

There are hills that pop up on these plains. The hills look rather like islands, and the plains look a bit like the sea. Here is a picture of what that is like.

Precious lived with her father, Obed, in a small house outside a village. Obed was a good, kind man who wore a rather battered old hat. That hat was well-known in the village and even further afield.

'Here he comes!' people would say when they saw his hat in the distance. 'Here comes Obed!'

On one occasion Obed lost his hat while walking home in the dark. A wind blew up and lifted it right off his head, and because there was no light he was unable to find it. The next day, when he went back to the place where he had lost the hat, there was still no sign of it. He searched and searched,

but without success.

'You could buy a new one, Daddy,' Precious suggested.

Obed shook his head. 'A new hat is never as comfortable as an old one,' he said. 'And I loved that hat.' He paused, looking up at his daughter. 'It saved my life, you know.'

Precious wondered how a hat could save your life. 'Please tell me about that,' she said. She loved her father's stories, especially when he told them at bedtime. There is something very exciting about a bedtime story, and it is even better if the story is told after the lights have been turned out. The words sound different, I think—as if they are being whispered just for you and for

nobody else. The words are all about you, like a warm blanket.

So Obed told her about the hat that evening, when it was already dark outside and the African sky was filling with stars.

'Quite a few years ago,' he began, 'before you were even born, I worked for a while on a farm. It was a very dry place, as there was not much rain in that part of the country. But each year the rains came, and the land would turn green as the plants returned to life. That could happen so quickly— sometimes overnight.

'My job was to see that the cattle were getting water to drink. We had boreholes to pump the water up from

deep wells. Then the cattle could slake their thirst from drinking troughs. I had to go and check that everything was working properly and fix it if it was not.

'Now, it was rather remote and empty down there, and although there were no lions, there were other wild animals—and birds. And this is all about one of those birds—a very dangerous bird.'

Precious interrupted him. 'Birds can't be dangerous,' she said, laughing at the thought. 'Birds are far too small.'

Obed shook his head. 'That's where you're wrong, my darling. There are some birds that are very big.'

'An eagle?' asked Precious.

'Bigger than that. Much bigger.'

She thought and thought, and was still thinking when Obed said: 'An ostrich!

'An ostrich,' her father went on, 'is much bigger than a man, and yes, it can be very dangerous. You have to be very careful if you get too close to an ostrich because they can kick. They have these very strong legs you see, and at the end

of one of them there is a claw. You can be very badly hurt by an ostrich kick— very, very badly hurt.'

Precious shivered. Sometimes her father's stories were a little bit frightening, even if they usually ended well.

'Now,' Obed continued, 'I was walking through the bush one day,

7

looking for some stray cattle, and suddenly I heard a noise. It was a very strange noise, and I stopped in my tracks wondering what it was. Then I saw it. Not far away from me, looking at me with those big angry eyes that they have, was an ostrich. And I knew right away that I had disturbed this creature and that it was about to attack me. The reason why it was so angry was that I had come too close to its nest. These birds make large nests on the ground in which they lay massive eggs. Think of a hen's egg. Then think of an egg twenty times bigger than that— that's an ostrich egg.

'Suddenly I remembered something I had been told, and it was just as well it came back to me. Looking down on the ground, I saw a long stick that had fallen from a nearby tree. I picked this up and put my hat on the end of this stick. Then I held it up high in the air— like this.

'Ostriches may be strong, but they are not very bright. I had remembered being told that if you put your hat on a stick and then held it up high, an ostrich would think that the hat was your head. They would also think that you were much taller than they were, and so they would leave you well alone. And, do you know, it worked! The ostrich saw my hat and thought I must be a very tall and strong creature— more than a match for her. So she backed off and I was able to continue on my way unkicked.'

Precious breathed a sigh of relief. She did not want her father to be kicked by an ostrich—who does?

'I'm glad it worked out well for you,' she said, as she drifted off to sleep.

'Thank you,' said her father. 'And now you go off to sleep, Precious, as you must be ready for school tomorrow morning.'

Precious closed her eyes and thought of school. She had heard that there was a new family coming to the school the next day—a boy and a girl—and she wondered what they would be like. New people are always interesting, and she thought that perhaps they might be her friends. It was good, she thought, to have old friends, but it was also good to have new ones.

But what about the hat? Did Obed

get it back after it had blown away? Yes, he did. It landed a long way away but when people picked it up they knew immediately whose it was, and it was returned to him a few days later none the worse for its adventure. Of course he was very pleased, and from that day onwards whenever there was a high wind, he held onto his hat very firmly. Which is what all of us should do, don't you think?

CHAPTER TWO

The next day Precious went to school eager to meet the two new arrivals. Neither of them was in her class, as one, the boy, was a year younger than she was, and his sister was a year older. But when the time came for the morning break, when the children spilled out of the classroom for half an hour of play, she quickly spotted them.

They were standing together under the shade of a tree. Precious noticed that they were watching the other children play, but not joining in. She understood that—she remembered what it was like to be new to a school. Everybody else seems to know lots of people, and you know none. It is not at all easy.

She made her way through the jostling knots of boys and girls until she reached the tree.

'Hello,' she said. 'My name's Precious.'

The girl smiled at her, and gave her

their names. 'I'm called Teb,' she said. 'And this is my brother, Pontsho.'

Pontsho looked at Precious a little warily, but when he saw her smile he smiled back.

'You're new, aren't you?' said Precious.

'Yes,' said the girl, glancing around her. 'And I don't know anybody.'

'Well,' said Precious. 'You know me now, don't you?'

The girl nodded.

'And I can tell you the names of everybody here,' said Precious, looking around the group of children. 'So I'm sure that you'll soon know everybody.'

They talked until it was time to go back into the classroom. Even when she was a young girl, Precious was very curious to find out as much as she could about other people. That was why she became such a good detective when she grew up—detectives have to keep their eyes open; they have to look at people and think *I wonder who that person is. I wonder where he comes from. I wonder what his favourite colour is.* And so on. She was very good at all that.

But of course one of the best ways of finding something out is to ask somebody. That was a rule that Precious Ramotswe learned very early in her life, and never forgot. So that morning, as she stood under the tree and talked to Teb and Pontsho, she found out a great deal about the two newcomers just by asking a few questions.

For instance, she asked: 'How many people live in your house?'

And Teb replied: 'There are six people who live in our house. There is me and my brother here—that's two. Then there's our mother, and our mother's sister. She is our aunt. And then there is our grandmother and our grandfather. They are very old. Our grandfather has no teeth left but our grandmother still has two or three. They like to sit in the sun all day and watch what's going on. They are very kind to us.'

And then Precious asked: 'What about your father?'

This time the boy answered. 'Our

Grandmother's
TEETH

father was struck by lightning two years ago,' he said.

'That's very sad,' said Precious.

The girl nodded. 'And so we had to sell the place we lived in. We moved here because my grandfather had a small house that he owned. We all live in that now.'

There were one or two other questions that Precious was able to ask. She asked how long it took them to walk to school, and they replied that it took just over half an hour. She asked them whether they believed in ghosts and Teb said no, although Pontsho hesitated a bit before he too said no. Then she asked them whether they liked apples, and Teb shook her head.

'I have never tasted an apple,' she said. 'Are they good?'

Precious tried not to show her surprise. Imagine never having tasted an apple! She herself loved apples, which her father bought her every Friday from one of the village stores. And then she saw something that she had not noticed before. Neither of the children was wearing shoes.

It did not take her long to work things out. Teb and Pontsho must be very poor. That was why they had never

tasted an apple and that was why they had no shoes. The thought made her sad. To walk to school for half an hour on ground that could become burning hot during the summer could not be easy. Of course your feet got used to it, and the skin underneath became harder and harder, but it must still have been uncomfortable. And what about thorns? Some of the bushes that grew at the side of paths were known for their vicious thorns. It would be only too easy to get one of these in your foot, and she knew how painful that could be.

She did not say anything, though. Sometimes people who are very poor are ashamed of it, even if they have no reason to be. Being poor is usually not

your fault, unless it's because you are very lazy. There are all sorts of reasons why people can be poor. They may have not been able to find any work. They may be in a job where they are not paid very much. They may have lost their father or mother because of illness or an accident or, Precious thought, lightning. Yes, lightning was the reason here, and it made her sad just to think of it.

The bell sounded for the end of the morning break. 'We have to go inside now,' said Precious. 'But if you like, I can walk home with you and we can talk a bit more. Your house isn't far from mine.'

'I would like that very much,' said Teb. And then she added: 'And if you come to my place, my brother can show you something really special.' She turned to Pontsho and gave him a warning look. 'But don't tell her yet, Pontsho! Let it be a surprise.'

'I won't tell,' said the boy. And smiled.

CHAPTER THREE

Precious could hardly contain her excitement on the walk to Teb's house. She wondered what her new friends could have in store for her, but try as she might, she could not guess what it was. That's the thing about a *real* surprise—you have no idea what it can possibly be, and the more you think about it, the harder it becomes to imagine what it is. Try it. Try to think of something that you don't know anything about. Hard, isn't it?

After they had been walking for a while Teb said: 'We're just about there.

Our house is just down there. See, near that hill? Where those trees are? That's our place.'

They were now outside the village, and there were no other buildings to be seen. There were plenty of trees, though, and it took Precious a few moments to work out which trees Teb meant. But then she saw a wisp of smoke rising up into the sky and she knew that this was from somebody's cooking fire. And, sure enough, when her eye followed the smoke down she saw that there was a small house tucked away at the end of it. So that was Teb's place.

They followed the path that led to the house and soon they were there.

'This is our place,' said Teb. 'This is where we live.'

Precious looked at the house. It was not very large and she wondered how everybody could fit inside. But she did not want to say anything about that, as people are usually proud of their houses and do not like other people (and that means us) to point out that their houses are too small, or too uncomfortable, or the wrong shape.

And so she said, "That's a nice house, Teb.'

That was not a lie. It is not a lie to say something nice to somebody. You have to remember that you can usually find something good to say about

anything if you look hard enough. And it's kind too, and Precious Ramotswe was a kind girl, as everybody knew.

Teb beamed with pleasure. 'Thank you,' she said. 'It's a bit small maybe, but then my brother sleeps out at the back, under a shelter, and so he doesn't take up much room. And my grandfather sleeps during the day and so he doesn't really need a bed at night—he just sits in his chair until morning. He's very happy, you know.'

Precious looked about her. In front of the house she saw two chairs, and in those two chairs she suddenly noticed that there were two very old people, both wearing hats that had been pulled down over their eyes.

'That's my grandfather and grandmother,' explained Teb. 'You

may think they can't see anything, with those hats pulled over their eyes, but they can. They have small holes in the hats, you see, and they see through those.'

Precious looked again, and saw that what Teb said was right. There were small holes in the hats and through those holes she could just make out . . . eyes.

And then one of the people raised a hand to wave to her, and then the other did the same thing. So Precious waved back.

Teb and Pontsho now took Precious to say hello to their grandparents. Precious did this, and was greeted very kindly.

'How do you do?' asked the grandfather. 'You are very welcome. Thank you for coming. Good day.'

And the grandmother said: 'How are you? It is very nice to see you. Good day too, my dear.'

Then Teb took her into the kitchen, which was the first room that you went

into when you entered the front door. There she met Teb's mother and her aunt, who were both busy crushing grain in a large tub. Some people don't know that bread comes from grain. You do, of course, but others have to be told that not everybody can go into a shop and buy a loaf of bread. Some people don't have shops anywhere near them, and some don't have the money to buy bread. So they have to make it. And it tastes delicious!

They went outside again, and it was now that Precious learned what the

Grain

big surprise was. And it was truly surprising. It was the sort of surprise that she would never have guessed, even if she had tried to do so for hours and hours.

What was this surprise? Well, here it is. It was a MEERKAT.

Now, what exactly is a meerkat? Well, it's not a cat. And it's not a squirrel, nor a racoon, nor a . . . Perhaps it's a mongoose, but it's easiest to think of them as being . . . just meerkats. They look like meerkats and they do the things that meerkats do— which is just what this meerkat now did, standing up on its hind legs, its front paws held out for balance, and its small black nose sniffing at the air with the greatest possible interest.

'A meerkat!' exclaimed Precious. 'You've got a meerkat!'

Teb smiled. 'Yes,' she said. 'This is Kosi. He belongs to my brother. His name means *chief*, you know.'

Precious leaned forward and, as she did so, the meerkat leaned forward too, his bright little eyes shining, his nose moist and glistening.

'He likes you,' said Pontsho. 'You can tell when he likes somebody.'

'And I like him too,' said Precious. 'Can I touch him?'

'Of course,' said Teb. 'Be gentle, though, as he can sometimes be a bit frightened.'

Precious reached forward and placed a finger as gently as she could on the back of the meerkat's head, as if to stroke him. His fur was smooth, a little bit like that of a well-groomed cat. It was a very strange feeling to be touching a meerkat.

Kosi half-turned his head when she touched him, but Precious could see that he was not in the least bit frightened.

'Where did you get him?' she asked.

Pontsho pointed to the hill behind the house.

'From the hill over there,' he said. 'I think he must have been separated from the rest of his family. He was sitting on one of the rocks, looking very lost. We call it Meerkat Hill now, because of him.'

'What does he eat?'

Pontsho smiled as he answered her question. 'He likes insects,' he said. 'He

loves worms. And he even likes to eat scorpions.'

Precious made a face. 'Scorpions!'

'Yes,' said Teb. 'He's very brave.'

'Brave enough to face up to a snake,' said Pontsho. 'Even a cobra.'

Precious drew in her breath. Cobras were very, very dangerous snakes and the thought that such a tiny creature as this could stand up to that deadly snake was hard to believe.

'Tell her,' said Teb. 'Tell Precious about the cobra.'

So they sat down, with Kosi sitting down beside them, as if he too was listening to the story that Pontsho then began.

CHAPTER FOUR

'This happened quite a long time ago,' began Pontsho.

'Last month,' said his sister, correcting him.

'Well, that's quite a long time ago,' said the boy. 'It didn't happen yesterday, did it?'

'It doesn't matter,' said Precious. 'I want to hear the story about the cobra. Just carry on with that.'

Pontsho began again. 'So,' he said, 'this happened quite a long time ago— last month. Our grandparents, as you know, like to sit in the sun. Sometimes they just sit and sleep, but sometimes they just sit. They've worked very hard all their lives, you see, and they're a bit tired now.

'Well, they were sitting there sleeping one afternoon. I had been off with Kosi to find some worms for his dinner that night. We found some very juicy-looking ones and his stomach was tight and full. He was very pleased with himself, I think.

'The moment I got back to the house, I noticed that something was wrong. Or at least I saw that something was different.'

Pontsho paused now, and looked at Precious, who was following his story wide-eyed. 'What was it?' she asked. 'What did you see?'

'My grandfather has big feet,' said Pontsho. 'When he sleeps he likes to take his shoes off, and so he had no shoes on. And do you know what I saw? I saw that a great big snake had curled himself round my grandfather's toes! Snakes like to do that, you know.

I think it keeps them warm. They love people's toes.'

Precious gasped. She did not like the idea of having a snake curled around *her* toes. 'Go on,' she urged. 'What happened next?'

'I wasn't sure what to do,' said Pontsho. 'For a little while I stood quite still with shock. You know how it is when you see something really frightening? You sometimes just stand there, unable to do anything. Well, that was how it was. And I was so shocked I forgot that I had Kosi with me.

'He had seen the snake too. He had been sitting on my shoulder, as he often likes to do when we go for a walk together. Now he jumped down and began to move very slowly towards my grandparents. Do you know how a cat will move when it's stalking a bird? That was how he moved. Very, very slowly, and very quietly.'

Precious drew in her breath. 'Did the snake see him?' she asked.

'Not to begin with,' answered Pontsho. 'But as he began to get closer and closer, the snake started to move.

It didn't move its coils—it just moved its head, which had bright black eyes like little pinpoints of dark light. And it put out its tongue, which came out like a tiny wet fork and then went back in. That's how snakes smell things, you know—they stick out their tongue and then take the smell back inside.

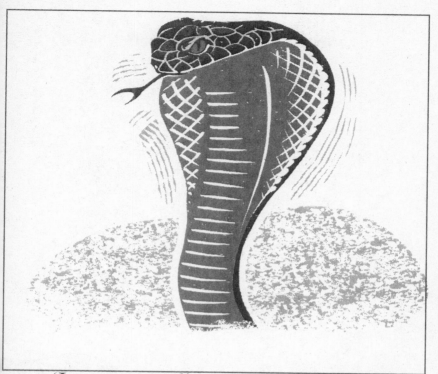

'I was really worried,' Pontsho continued. 'If the snake became angry, then he could very easily bite my grandfather. And if that happened, then there would be very little we could do for him. A cobra injects poison through his fangs and it stops you breathing and makes your heart stop too. My grandfather would never wake up if that happened. It would be the end of him.

'But then something really amazing

happened. Kosi began to scratch at the ground as if he was looking for a worm, or even a scorpion. I could hardly believe it. Why would he suddenly be hungry after eating all those juicy worms we had found? But then I understood what he was doing. He was attracting the attention of the snake.

'The snake moved his head again. He was watching the meerkat and he was clearly thinking: "Now there's a tasty little creature that would go very nicely down my throat!" A big snake, like a cobra, loves to eat meerkats—if he can catch them.

'Very slowly, the cobra began to unwind himself from my grandfather's feet. Very smoothly, like a long piece of hosepipe, he moved across the ground towards Kosi. I stood quite still,

although I was terrified that Kosi was going to be caught by the snake. I love him so much, you know, and I would never find another meerkat if anything happened to him.

'The next thing I knew was that Kosi had jumped up in the air. This happened at exactly the moment that the cobra struck at him. He missed, of course, and his fangs ended biting the ground rather than a meerkat arm or leg. Kosi was safe, and now he ran helter-skelter towards some thick grass with the snake sliding after him, its hood up in anger.

'Ten minutes later, Kosi came back unharmed. He had led the snake off into the grass and left him there. The snake never returned.'

'And what did your grandfather

think?' asked Precious.

'He had been asleep all along,' said Teb. 'So he didn't mind. But he was very grateful to Kosi, of course. "Take good care of that meerkat," he said to Pontsho.'

'And I do,' said the boy. 'I really do.'

Precious smiled, and tickled the meerkat under his chin, just as she had seen Pontsho do. The tiny creature liked that, it seemed, closing his eyes with pleasure. He was so small, thought Precious, and yet he had been brave enough to lure away a fully-grown cobra. Small and brave, she thought. Small and brave.

CHAPTER FIVE

Precious thought a lot about Kosi over the next few days. Whenever she saw Pontsho at school she would ask him how the meerkat was, and he would tell her of Kosi's latest adventures. He had caught a large scorpion, he said, or he had stolen a piece of bread from the kitchen, or had done some other thing that meerkats like to do. One of these things, Pontsho told her, was to ride on the back of the family's cow. 'He loves doing that,' said Pontsho. 'He sits on the cow's back for hours, looking out over everything. It's his favourite place, I think.'

Precious smiled at this and said she hoped that she would have the chance to see him again soon.

'Perhaps you will,' said Pontsho, and winked.

She was to find out what that wink meant a few days later. Going outside during the morning break, she saw Pontsho beckoning her.

She went to join him. 'Yes?' she said. 'Did you want something, Pontsho?'

He drew her aside. 'He's here,' he whispered.

Precious was puzzled. 'Who's here?'

'Your friend,' said Pontsho, pointing to his school bag. 'Kosi.'

Precious looked down at the bag. To her astonishment, she saw a small nose sticking out of one corner, sniffing the air. Pontsho had brought Kosi to school.

She was excited, but at the same time she was more than a little bit worried. 'You'll get into trouble,' she warned.

Pontsho shook his head. 'Nobody will find out,' he said. 'He wanted to come, you see. He'll be good.'

No sooner had he said that than he was proved quite wrong. Somehow Kosi managed to get the top of the bag undone. Then, with a wiggle and a twist—the sort of movement that only meerkats can manage—he was out of the bag. Precious gasped as the meerkat, looking about him with interest, thought about what to do next. And then she gasped again—more loudly this time—when the tiny creature decided to dash off across the playground and head straight for the one place she hoped he would not go: the teachers' room.

This room was beside the classrooms and it was where the teachers went to drink tea while the children played outside. Its door was always left

open, so that the teachers could see if anybody got up to mischief outside. But that meant that for a meerkat, looking around for somewhere to go, it seemed like a very good place to investigate.

As Kosi vanished into the teachers' room, Pontsho and Precious ran behind him, stopping short of the door itself, but standing where they could see what was happening inside. It was a very funny sight, but one that still made Precious and Pontsho hold their breath in alarm.

Entering the room, all that Kosi must have seen was legs—a whole forest of legs. Now for a meerkat,

there is nothing more interesting than legs. From the meerkat point of view, legs are trees, and trees, as every meerkat knows, are for climbing up. That gives them a better view of what is happening in the long grass around them. Every meerkat is taught that and every meerkat remembers it.

Kosi made his way cautiously around the legs and ankles. Now and then he stopped, and would fiddle with a shoe-lace or gingerly touch a bony ankle; now and then he would dodge out of the way if a foot was suddenly moved. But then, finding a pair of particularly stout legs, he stopped and looked up.

These legs were clearly very interesting to him, and he appeared to be unsure as to whether or not to climb them. They looked very much like trees to Kosi—even if they were, in fact, the legs of the Principal of the school, a rather strict man who did not like it at all when anybody did something wrong.

'Oh no,' groaned Pontsho, as he saw what was happening.

Kosi took a step forward and took hold of the principal's trousers. Up above, the Principal felt something, and perhaps thought that a fly, or even maybe a spider, had landed on him and would need to be brushed off. He was

busy talking to one of the teachers at the time, and so he just leant forward, without looking what he was doing, and brushed the fly away.

Kosi saw the Principal's hand approaching him and did what any meerkat would do. He leapt up as high as he could—and landed on the head of the teacher sitting next to the Principal. In nature, meerkats will always seek the highest or the lowest point when they are worried. The highest point gives them a good view of approaching danger, and the lowest point gives them refuge.

The teacher screamed. She had no

idea what was perched on the top of her head as she could not see what it was. But the other teachers could, and they all cried out.

'He's on your head!' they shouted.

And then they started to laugh. It was, of course, a very funny sight, and although we shouldn't laugh at people, there are times when it's impossible to keep the laughter in.

Happily, the teacher herself imagined how funny she must have looked, and began to laugh too.

Pontsho felt that there was only one thing to do. He knew that it would get him into trouble, but he had to retrieve Kosi from the teacher's head. So he stepped forward, into the teacher's room, and called Kosi to him.

Seeing Pontsho, Kosi straightaway jumped off the teacher's head and scampered across the room to his owner.

'Young man,' said the Principal sternly, 'you have a lot of explaining to do.'

Pontsho said he was sorry. He knew that nobody was allowed to bring animals to school, and he would not do it again.

The Principal looked at him. He was frowning, and Pontsho knew

that he was going to get into deep trouble. But then, quite suddenly, the Principal stopped frowning and a broad smile appeared on his face.

'Well,' he said, 'the rules say that nobody can bring a dog to school. They also say something about not bringing mice or other pets like that. But they don't say anything about meerkats, do they?'

'No,' said one of the teachers, beginning to laugh. 'They don't.'

The Principal raised a finger. 'That's not to say that the rules won't say that in the future,' he said. 'But for today, I think it will be all right.'

Pontsho looked at Precious with relief. She was standing at the door watching what was happening, and she was smiling too.

'You should tell us a bit more about this funny little creature,' said the Principal. 'Come on—don't be shy.'

52

So Pontsho told the teachers all about Kosi and about how he had saved his grandfather. At the end of this tale, the teachers all crowded round and were allowed to pat Kosi gently on the head.  Pontsho swelled with pride, as did Precious, and, I think, little Kosi did too. Meerkats like attention. They like people to pat them on the head and say nice things. Rather like the rest of us, don't you think?

CHAPTER SIX

Kosi's visit to school ended well but then, a few days later, when school had just finished for the day and Precious was starting her walk home, she came across Teb sitting by the side of the road—and she was crying. There was no sign of Pontsho.

'What's wrong?' she asked, putting her arm around her friend's shoulder.

For a little while Teb was sobbing too much to answer, but then she turned to Precious and told her. 'Our cow,' she said, 'is going to have a calf. But she wandered off yesterday and she hasn't come back. Pontsho stayed at home today to help call her.' Precious said she was very sorry to hear this news. She understood how important that cow was to Teb's family. It was just about everything they had. And when the calf was born that would be important too, as they could sell that to somebody and use the money to pay for food.

Teb dried her tears. 'My mother doesn't know what to do,' she said. 'We've called her and called her, but we have no idea where she's gone. Sometimes cows do that, my grandfather said. He told me that cows just wander off and never return.'

Precious thought hard. She had already decided, even at her age, that when she grew up she would be a detective, and now here was a case right in front of her that needed solving.

'Can I help?' she asked gently.

Teb turned to her. 'Could you?' she asked.

'Yes,' said Precious. But even as she spoke, she wondered what she could possibly do to solve the mystery of the missing cow. But, after a moment or two, it came to her. Had they looked for tracks? When cows walk on the ground, they leave hoof-prints where they have been. Had Teb or Pontsho looked for these?

Teb shook her head.

'Then we should do so,' said Precious. 'I'll come home with you now and we can start to look for tracks.'

Teb immediately brightened. 'My mother will be very pleased if we find her,' she said. 'She'll make us all a reward of fat cakes!'

Precious loved fat cakes, which are a delicious type of fried doughnut that are very popular in Botswana. But she did not like to think of a reward just yet. It was all very well having an idea, but as every detective knows only too well, not all ideas solve the case.

When they reached the house, Pontsho ran out to meet them. At first they thought he might be bringing good news, but when they saw his face, they realised that this was not so.

'We've called and called,' he said hoarsely. 'But we haven't found her.'

Teb told him about the idea that Precious had come up with. Pontsho thought for a moment and then nodded. 'Let's look,' he said.

They led Precious to the place where the cow had last been seen. This was a small clearing at the bottom of Meerkat Hill, right behind the family's house. There was a fence, but it was an old one, and it would have been very easy for a cow just to step over it if she really wanted to.

Precious started to walk round the fence, taking great care not to disturb the ground. Detectives always do that, as you probably know: they don't want to destroy any of the clues that may be lying around. And here was one, right in front of her.

'Over here,' she called, pointing to the ground in front of her.

Teb and Pontsho ran over to join her.

'This is where she went,' said Precious. 'Look. There are the marks of her hooves.'

Teb and Pontsho peered down at the tracks in the dusty soil.

'Now,' said Precious. 'If we follow them, we'll see where she went.'

They set off, and everybody was very excited. So excited were they, in fact, that they did not notice that they had been joined by Kosi, who was following behind them, his little nose twitching with interest.

Fortunately it had not rained.

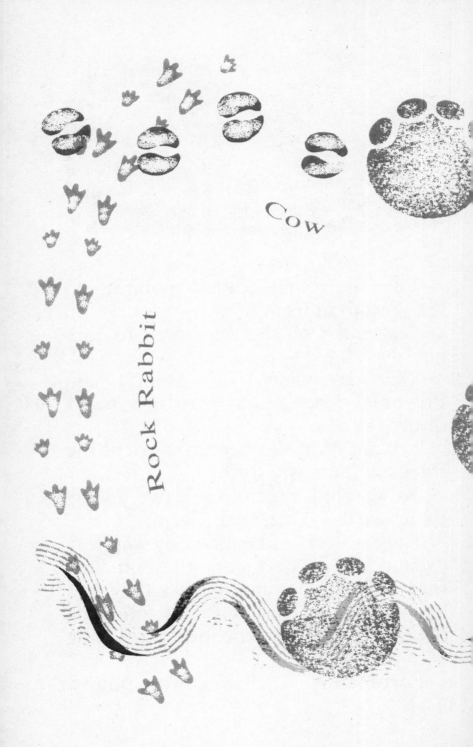

Cow

Rock Rabbit

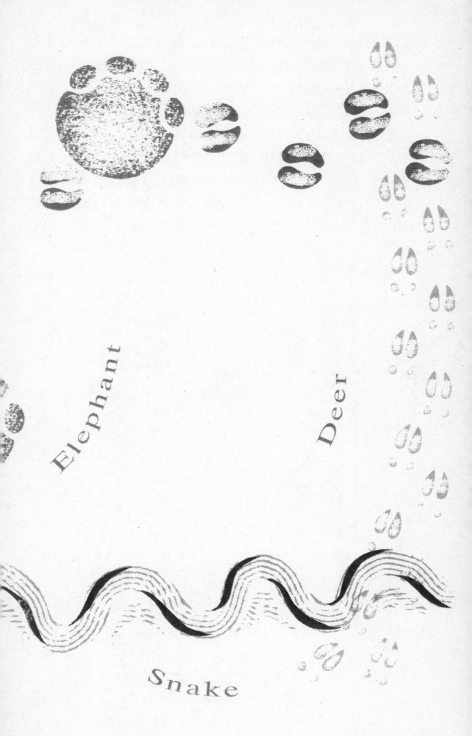

Elephant

Deer

Snake

Botswana is a dry country, and the rain only comes in what they call the rainy season—those few months when the sky fills with heavy purple thunder-clouds and the thirsty country waits expectantly for the first drops. Had it rained, then the hoof-prints they were following would have been washed away in the deluge. As it was, they were

still firm and clear, even if here and there they were mixed up with the hoof-prints of smaller animals. It was easy, though, for Precious to tell the difference between the marks that a cow's hoof makes and the marks made by a small deer, or a rock rabbit, or something like that.

Pontsho had now spotted Kosi and had invited him to travel on his shoulder. The meerkat liked that, and sat importantly on his vantage point, as if it was he who was the detective and not Precious Ramotswe. Well, as we will shortly find out, there was some truth in that, but for now here they are, all following the tracks, the heart of each of them filled with hope that they would soon find the missing cow.

CHAPTER SEVEN

The cow had wandered a long way. At times, when she had crossed stony ground, the tracks became faint, and Precious had to get down on her hands and knees to see them. At other times, though, the cow had made her way over bare sandy soil, and the hoof-prints were very easily visible.

They had been walking for well over an hour and were beginning to wonder whether they would ever catch up with the cow when Pontsho suddenly called out.

'Over there!' he shouted. 'Look!'

They stopped and stared in the direction in which he was pointing. For a moment or two Precious could not make out what it was that had attracted the boy's attention, but then she saw it. A large herd of cattle was gathered beside a rough dirt road that ran through the scrub bush.

Pontsho whistled. 'Look how many there are,' he said. 'I wonder what's

going on.'

Precious knew the answer to that. Her father knew a lot about cattle, and had once taken her to see a herd being prepared for market. This was what was happening here: a farmer had gathered in all his cattle to be collected for market. Unfortunately the cow must have heard or smelled them and had decided to join them. After all, if you are a cow and you see lots of other cows getting together, you must think: why shouldn't I be there too?

The three children ran towards the herd. They had seen a couple of men standing nearby and they imagined that these were the people in charge. All

they would have to do was to identify their cow and then lead her back to her home.

It was Teb who spoke first.

'Excuse me,' she said very politely. 'Our cow has run away. We've tracked her and we think she's joined this herd. Could we have her back please?'

The two men, who had been talking to one another, stopped their conversation and looked at Teb.

'These are our cows,' one said. 'Sorry. Your cow must have gone somewhere else.'

'No,' said Precious. 'She's here. We followed her hoof-prints.'

One of the men laughed. 'Followed

her hoof-prints? What nonsense! These cows all belong to us.'

Precious bit her lip. It was hard not to be believed when you know that you're telling the truth. But there is no point in getting cross about it, because that can only make it worse. So instead of insisting that she was right, she simply said to the men, 'But if we could prove it? Would you let us take our cow?'

Both men nodded. 'Of course,' one said. Then he added, 'But I really don't see how you're going to do that. All these cattle look the same, you know.'

With a sinking heart, Precious saw that this was so—all the cows were more or less the same colour—reddish-brown. But then, without having to think about it, she had an idea. It was the second good idea that had come to her that day, and she lost no time in explaining it to Teb and Pontsho.

'Listen,' she said, dropping her voice so that the men could not hear her. 'Do you think that Kosi would know your cow, even in a big herd?'

It was Pontsho who answered. 'Of

course,' he said. 'He loves to ride on her back, as I told you. They're very good friends.'

This was the answer Precious had been hoping for. 'Right,' she said. 'Let's ask him to find her.'

Kosi frowned. 'How will we do that?'

Precious looked at the meerkat, who was sitting on Pontsho's shoulder watching the restless herd of cows with interest. 'Ask him,' she said. 'Meerkats are good at understanding things. He might be able to do it.'

Then she turned to the men. 'Excuse

me,' she said. 'This meerkat knows my friends' cow very well. If he can find her, will you let us take her home?'

The men laughed. 'Of course,' said one of them. 'Of course we'll let you take her home. But how is a tiny little meerkat going to find one cow in a large herd like this? It won't happen, will it?'

Precious did not answer that question, but turned to Pontsho. 'Ask him, Pontsho,' she said.

Pontsho took Kosi off his shoulder and put him down on the ground. 'Find your friend,' he whispered. 'Find her!'

The meerkat got up on its hind legs and looked at Pontsho enquiringly. Then he turned his nose towards

the herd of cows and sniffed at the air. Precious held her breath. Was it possible that the meerkat understood what was expected of him?

And then, with a sudden little jump—a hop of the sort that meerkats perform when they have some task to do—Kosi scurried off into the herd, weaving and dodging to keep out of the way of the cows' hooves. From where Precious was standing, it looked very dangerous—and it was. At one point she thought that Kosi would be crushed, but he proved too nimble for that, and managed to avoid being stamped upon.

When the meerkat reached the centre of the herd he seemed to

disappear for a moment. But then he suddenly popped up again, and now he was riding on the back of one of the cows. 'That's her!' shouted Teb. 'See! That's her.'

Precious turned to the men. 'Do you see that?' she asked. 'You wanted proof—well there it is. The meerkat has found her friend.'

The men may have been a bit gruff, but they were not ones to break their promise. They had said that if the meerkat found the cow, then the children could take her home. And so they set about rounding up Teb's cow, who still had a meerkat perched on her back.

'You can take her home, I suppose,' said one of the men. And then, even if a bit reluctantly, he added, 'And well done, whoever it was who came up with that idea!'

Precious said nothing. She did not like to boast, and the fact that the family had recovered their cow was more than enough reward for her.

CHAPTER EIGHT

They led the cow home, guiding her gently along the path they had followed to find her. When they reached the bottom of Meerkat Hill, Precious could see the two grandparents waving their hands excitedly. They were soon joined by Teb's mother and the aunt, both of whom joined in the energetic waving.

'This is a miracle,' said the grandfather as he ran forwards to welcome the returning cow. He could not run very fast, as his legs were a bit bent and spindly, but he did his best, and was soon stroking the cow on the side of her neck, whispering into her ear the sort of things people say to cows who have been away but who have come back.

'This is wonderful,' said Teb's mother. 'I think you all deserve a reward for finding our cow.'

Teb glanced at Precious, and smiled. Then she turned to her mother and asked, 'Fat cakes?'

Her mother nodded. 'I shall make them immediately, even if it's almost time for our evening meal.'

The mention of evening made Precious look at the sun, which was now beginning to drop down in the sky. 'I'll have to get home soon,' she said. 'My father will be beginning to get worried.'

Teb looked imploringly at her mother. 'Can't Precious stay?' she asked.

'I could go and ask her father,' said the aunt. 'I have to go to the store, and I could call at their house and ask him if Precious can stay overnight.'

Both Teb and Pontsho thought this

was a very good idea, as did Precious herself of course, and the aunt lost no time in setting off on her mission. By the time the fat cakes were ready and sprinkled with sugar, the aunt had come back to announce that Obed had said that it was perfectly all right for his daughter to stay overnight at Teb's house.

They sat and ate the fat cakes. There were two each for everybody, which was more than enough, as the grandparents could not finish theirs and passed them on. The children kindly finished them for them, and then everybody licked their fingers to get the last of the sugar and stickiness off. The last bits of everything taste particularly good, don't you find?

By now it was beginning to get dark. The sun in Africa sinks rather quickly. The sky turns a coppery gold colour and then down beyond the horizon goes the great red ball of the sun. As soon as it is gone, the sky becomes light blue again and then dark blue, and the stars appear—great silver fields of them.

Since it was a special occasion, the grandfather made a fire outside for Teb, Pontsho and Precious to sit around. Then he moved his chair to the fire too, and told them a story of how things were a long time ago, when he was a boy. They listened, and then, after he had finished and had moved his chair back to its usual place, they talked among themselves.

There was much to talk about. They remembered all about following the cow's hoof-prints and Pontsho thought that he would try his skill at tracking other animals in future, now that Precious had shown him how to do it. Teb thought this was a good idea, and

said that she would practise looking
for clues, just as Precious had done.
'You never know what you might find,'
she remarked. 'There are all sorts of
mysteries once you start to look for
them.'

Precious agreed. She had only been
a detective for a short time, but she
had already solved two important
mysteries—one in which monkeys
played a part, and this one involving a
meerkat and a cow. There were bound
to be others, she thought.

'You're very lucky to be such a good
detective,' said Pontsho.

Precious smiled modestly. She never
boasted, but she was glad that she had

discovered the thing that she seemed to be really good at. Most people can do at least one thing rather well, but sometimes it takes a bit of time to find out what that thing is. She had found it, and now that she had done so, she would be able to use that talent well. Many years later, she would become a famous detective—the first lady detective in Botswana—but that, of course, is a story that we shall hear about much later on.

Although they had very much enjoyed the fat cakes, there was still enough room for their normal dinner, although nobody needed very large helpings that night. Then, after the meal, it was time for them to go to bed. Pontsho went off to his shelter at the back of the house, and Precious and Teb each laid out a sleeping mat in the corner of the kitchen where Teb normally slept. Teb's mother lent Precious a spare blanket so that she could wrap herself up and keep warm for the night. Although Botswana is a hot country, the nights themselves can be cold, as they often are in deserts and other warm places.

As she lay there in the darkness, thinking of the events of the day, Precious felt happy that everything had worked out so well. The cow was safely back and in due course she would have her calf. In fact, although nobody knew it at the time, the cow was due to have twins. That was very welcome news for the family, as it meant that they would have two calves to sell rather than one. And it meant, too, that they would be able to buy shoes for Teb and Pontsho, which was a very good thing.

Teb must have been very tired, as she dropped off to sleep almost straightaway. Precious, though, remained awake a bit longer, and she was still awake when a small furry creature crept through the door and made his way to where she was lying.

The first thing she knew of him was the feel of his tiny moist nose sniffing at her cheek.

She did not say anything to Kosi, as she did not want to wake Teb. So she simply stroked the tiny meerkat gently and allowed him to cuddle up to her. He was tired too, and after a few minutes she felt his breathing change and she knew he was asleep. In nature, meerkats sleep together in a burrow they make underground. They lie with their tiny arms about one another—a whole family of meerkats—safe and sound in their underground house. Above them, in the moonlight, there

are all sorts of dangers—owls and snakes and other enemies—but they are safe down below, huddled together for warmth.

Precious drifted off to sleep eventually. She dreamed that night of cows and meerkats and tracks in the sand. She dreamed, too, of fat cakes and happy people and of her friends and of how good it felt to have been able to help them. Because helping other people *is* a good thing, whether or not you are a detective.

And in the morning, do you know, Kosi was still there, his paws under his chin, his bright black eyes closed. But the sun came up, floating slowly up into the sky, and all three of them awoke at much the same time when the kitchen filled with light.

'Another day,' said Teb, rubbing the sleep from her eyes.

'Yes,' said Precious, sitting up on her sleeping mat. 'Another day.'

And Kosi, of course, said nothing, but as Precious looked at the tiny meerkat, she was sure that he was smiling.